Contents

Introduction

When typing copy or arranging the pages for the local church newsletter, the secretary or editor often winds up with two to four lines of space to fill on a page or at the bottom of a column. These tiny areas of space are too small for most clip-art spots now available to churches. This book is designed to fill this very practical need. It provides mini-fillers for local church editors to clip and publish in these small areas of white space.

Each mini-filler appears in four different formats to give you the exact size and arrangement you are likely to need for your newsletter or worship bulletin. Each mini-filler is also boxed for your convenience. All you have to do is clip the size you need and paste it on your newsletter layout sheet.

My thanks to church secretaries and church newsletter editors who have suggested the need for this book. My hope is that it will help you produce a more interesting and informative publication for the members of your church.

George W. Knight

1

Gems of Wisdom

The trouble with many self-made people is, they didn't finish the job.

Unfinished Task
The trouble with many self-made people is, they didn't finish the job.

The trouble with many self-made people is, they didn't finish the job.

Unfinished Task
The trouble with many self-made people is, they didn't finish the job.

It's not how old you are, but how you are old.

How Are You Old?
It's not how old you are, but how you are old.

It's not how old you are, but how you are old.

How Are You Old?
It's not how old you are, but how you are old.

The cross is the only
ladder high enough to
touch heaven.

Upward Reach
The cross is the only
ladder high enough to
touch heaven.

The cross is the only ladder high enough to touch heaven.

Upward Reach
The cross is the only ladder high enough to touch heaven.

Ideas are stubborn; they
won't work unless you do.

Working Ideas
Ideas are stubborn; they
won't work unless you do.

Ideas are stubborn; they won't work unless you do.

Working Ideas
Ideas are stubborn; they won't work unless you do.

About the time you learn to
make the most of life, most
of it is gone.

Like a Vapor
About the time you learn to
make the most of life, most
of it is gone.

About the time you learn to make the
most of life, most of it is gone.

Like a Vapor
About the time you learn to make the
most of life, most of it is gone.

One of the tough things about business is minding your own.

Hard to Do
One of the tough things about business is minding your own.

One of the tough things about business is minding your own.

Hard to Do
One of the tough things about business is minding your own.

Success is getting what you want; happiness is wanting what you get.

A Matter of Wants
Success is getting what you want; happiness is wanting what you get.

Success is getting what you want; happiness is wanting what you get.

A Matter of Wants
Success is getting what you want; happiness is wanting what you get.

The dictionary is the only place where success comes before work.

S Before W
The dictionary is the only place where success comes before work.

The dictionary is the only place where success comes before work.

S Before W
The dictionary is the only place where success comes before work.

What kind of church would my church be if every member were just like me?

Good Question
What kind of church would my church be if every member were just like me?

What kind of church would my church be if every member were just like me?

Good Question
What kind of church would my church be if every member were just like me?

Be careful of your thoughts; they could break into words at any time.

Watch Out!
Be careful of your thoughts; they could break into words at any time.

Be careful of your thoughts; they could break into words at any time.

Watch Out!
Be careful of your thoughts; they could break into words at any time.

A modest person is one who doesn't blow his knows.

Modesty Defined
A modest person is one who doesn't blow his knows.

A modest person is one who doesn't blow his knows.

Modesty Defined
A modest person is one who doesn't blow his knows.

Minds are like
parachutes; they function
best when fully open.

Parachute Minds
Minds are like
parachutes; they function
best when fully open.

Minds are like parachutes; they function best when fully open.

Parachute Minds
Minds are like parachutes; they function best when fully open.

A little smile adds a lot
to your face value.

Value of a Smile
A little smile adds a lot
to your face value.

A little smile adds a lot to your face value.

Value of a Smile
A little smile adds a lot to your face value.

The faith that removes
mountains always
carries a pick.

Working Faith
The faith that removes
mountains always
carries a pick.

The faith that removes mountains always carries a pick.

Working Faith
The faith that removes mountains always carries a pick.

15

Be true to your convictions, but make sure your convictions are true.

True Convictions
Be true to your convictions, but make sure your convictions are true.

Be true to your convictions, but make sure your convictions are true.

True Convictions
Be true to your convictions, but make sure your convictions are true.

The easiest person in the world to deceive is yourself.

Self-Deception
The easiest person in the world to deceive is yourself.

The easiest person in the world to deceive is yourself.

Self-Deception
The easiest person in the world to deceive is yourself.

It's good to flee temptation—but don't leave a forwarding address.

Address Unknown
It's good to flee temptation—but don't leave a forwarding address.

It's good to flee temptation—but don't leave a forwarding address.

Address Unknown
It's good to flee temptation—but don't leave a forwarding address.

Those who hold a conver-
sation should let go of it
now and then.

Turn It Loose!
Those who hold a conver-
sation should let go of it
now and then.

Those who hold a conversation should
let go of it now and then.

Turn It Loose!
Those who hold a conversation should
let go of it now and then.

Some minds are like
concrete—all mixed up and
permanently set.

Hardened State
Some minds are like
concrete—all mixed up and
permanently set.

Some minds are like concrete—all
mixed up and permanently set.

Hardened State
Some minds are like concrete—all
mixed up and permanently set.

There's a big difference
between having to say
something and having
something to say.

What a Difference!
There's a big difference
between having to say
something and having
something to say.

There's a big difference between having to say
something and having something to say.

What a Difference!
There's a big difference between having to say
something and having something to say.

Remember that those who least deserve love probably need it the most.

Most Deserving
Remember that those who least deserve love probably need it the most.

Remember that those who least deserve love probably need it the most.

Most Deserving
Remember that those who least deserve love probably need it the most.

One good thing about the future is that it comes one day at a time.

Day by Day
One good thing about the future is that it comes one day at a time.

One good thing about the future is that it comes one day at a time.

Day by Day
One good thing about the future is that it comes one day at a time.

Drive so your driver's license will expire before you do.

Good Advice
Drive so your driver's license will expire before you do.

Drive so your driver's license will expire before you do.

Good Advice
Drive so your driver's license will expire before you do.

Keep your words sweet;
you may have to eat them.

Sweet Words
Keep your words sweet;
you may have to eat them.

Keep your words sweet; you may have to eat them.

Sweet Words
Keep your words sweet; you may have to eat them.

If you think you have no
faults—that's another one to
add to the list!

One More
If you think you have no
faults—that's another one to
add to the list!

If you think you have no faults—that's
another one to add to the list!

One More
If you think you have no faults—that's
another one to add to the list!

It's what we learn after we
think we know it all that
really counts.

Valuable Lessons
It's what we learn after we
think we know it all that
really counts.

It's what we learn after we think we
know it all that really counts.

Valuable Lessons
It's what we learn after we think we
know it all that really counts.

23

It's twice as hard to crush a half-truth as an outright lie.

Hard to Crush
It's twice as hard to crush a half-truth as an outright lie.

It's twice as hard to crush a half-truth as an outright lie.

Hard to Crush
It's twice as hard to crush a half-truth as an outright lie.

A smooth sea never made a successful sailor.

Rough Sea
A smooth sea never made a successful sailor.

A smooth sea never made a successful sailor.

Rough Sea
A smooth sea never made a successful sailor.

The smallest deed is better than the largest intention.

When Small Is Best
The smallest deed is better than the largest intention.

The smallest deed is better than the largest intention.

When Small Is Best
The smallest deed is better than the largest intention.

25

It's better to be despised for doing right than praised for doing wrong.

A Just Cause
It's better to be despised for doing right than praised for doing wrong.

It's better to be despised for doing right than praised for doing wrong.

A Just Cause
It's better to be despised for doing right than praised for doing wrong.

Even if the teeth are false, let the tongue be true.

Straight Tongue
Even if the teeth are false, let the tongue be true.

Even if the teeth are false, let the tongue be true.

Straight Tongue
Even if the teeth are false, let the tongue be true.

Remember, the brook would lose its song if you took the rocks away.

Singing Brook
Remember, the brook would lose its song if you took the rocks away.

Remember, the brook would lose its song if you took the rocks away.

Singing Brook
Remember, the brook would lose its song if you took the rocks away.

Don't pray for an easy life;
ask God to make you a
stronger person.

Pray for Strength
Don't pray for an easy life;
ask God to make you a
stronger person.

Don't pray for an easy life; ask God
to make you a stronger person.

Pray for Strength
Don't pray for an easy life; ask God
to make you a stronger person.

Too many things we wait
for turn out to be not
worth the delay.

Not Worth the Wait
Too many things we wait
for turn out to be not
worth the delay.

Too many things we wait for turn out to be not worth the delay.

Not Worth the Wait
Too many things we wait for turn out to be not worth the delay.

If you must kill time, try
working it to death.

Overwork
If you must kill time, try
working it to death.

If you must kill time, try working it to death.

Overwork
If you must kill time, try working it to death.

29

The best way to save
face is to keep the lower
half firmly shut.

How to Save Face
The best way to save
face is to keep the lower
half firmly shut.

The best way to save face is to keep the lower half firmly shut.

How to Save Face
The best way to save face is to keep the lower half firmly shut.

Truth does not need
defenders; it is better
served by witnesses.

Witnesses Needed
Truth does not need
defenders; it is better
served by witnesses.

Truth does not need defenders; it
is better served by witnesses.

Witnesses Needed
Truth does not need defenders; it
is better served by witnesses.

The Christian steward who
gives when asked has
waited too long.

No Need to Wait
The Christian steward who
gives when asked has
waited too long.

The Christian steward who gives when
asked has waited too long.

No Need to Wait
The Christian steward who gives when
asked has waited too long.

Most people who wake up famous haven't been asleep.

Not Napping
Most people who wake up famous haven't been asleep.

Most people who wake up famous haven't been asleep.

Not Napping
Most people who wake up famous haven't been asleep.

The person who has a right to boast doesn't have to.

Unclaimed Right
The person who has a right to boast doesn't have to.

The person who has a right to boast doesn't have to.

Unclaimed Right
The person who has a right to boast doesn't have to.

Good example is more than twice as valuable as good advice.

Good Example
Good example is more than twice as valuable as good advice.

Good example is more than twice as valuable as good advice.

Good Example
Good example is more than twice as valuable as good advice.

33

If you can't find the bright
side, polish the dull side.

Spit and Polish
If you can't find the bright
side, polish the dull side.

If you can't find the bright side, polish the dull side.

Spit and Polish
If you can't find the bright side, polish the dull side.

It's useless to wait for your
ship to come in if you didn't
send one out.

Fruitless Wait
It's useless to wait for your
ship to come in if you didn't
send one out.

It's useless to wait for your ship to come
in if you didn't send one out.

Fruitless Wait
It's useless to wait for your ship to come
in if you didn't send one out.

The easiest thing in the
world to mind is your
neighbor's business.

Easy Work
The easiest thing in the
world to mind is your
neighbor's business.

The easiest thing in the world to mind
is your neighbor's business.

Easy Work
The easiest thing in the world to mind
is your neighbor's business.

Tact is the art of making a point without developing an enemy.

Tact Defined
Tact is the art of making a point without developing an enemy.

Tact is the art of making a point without developing an enemy.

Tact Defined
Tact is the art of making a point without developing an enemy.

Truth hurts. You would too if you were kicked around that much.

Suffering Truth
Truth hurts. You would too if you were kicked around that much.

Truth hurts. You would too if you were kicked around that much.

Suffering Truth
Truth hurts. You would too if you were kicked around that much.

Experience is what allows you to recognize a mistake the second time you make it.

You Look Familiar
Experience is what allows you to recognize a mistake the second time you make it.

Experience is what allows you to recognize a mistake the second time you make it.

You Look Familiar
Experience is what allows you to recognize a mistake the second time you make it.

37

Few people blame themselves until they have exhausted all other possibilities.

No One Else
Few people blame themselves until they have exhausted all other possibilities.

Few people blame themselves until they have exhausted all other possibilities.

No One Else
Few people blame themselves until they have exhausted all other possibilities.

The only thing more expensive than education is ignorance.

High Cost
The only thing more expensive than education is ignorance.

The only thing more expensive than education is ignorance.

High Cost
The only thing more expensive than education is ignorance.

It's much wiser to choose what you say than to say what you choose.

The Wiser Choice
It's much wiser to choose what you say than to say what you choose.

It's much wiser to choose what you say than to say what you choose.

The Wiser Choice
It's much wiser to choose what you say than to say what you choose.

Almost any system will work
if the people behind it do.

Work the Plan
Almost any system will work
if the people behind it do.

Almost any system will work if the people behind it do.

Work the Plan
Almost any system will work if the people behind it do.

Be content with what
you have but never with
what you are.

Contentment
Be content with what
you have but never with
what you are.

Be content with what you have but never with what you are.

Contentment
Be content with what you have but never with what you are.

If at first you don't
succeed—you're
running about average.

Law of Averages
If at first you don't
succeed—you're
running about average.

If at first you don't succeed—you're running about average.

Law of Averages
If at first you don't succeed—you're running about average.

What a person possesses
is not as important as
what possesses him.

Owner or Ownee?
What a person possesses
is not as important as what
possesses him.

What a person possesses is not as
important as what possesses him.

Owner or Ownee?
What a person possesses is not as
important as what possesses him.

If you don't have Christ-
mas in your heart, you
won't find it under a tree.

Search Within
If you don't have Christ-
mas in your heart, you
won't find it under a tree.

If you don't have Christmas in your heart,
you won't find it under a tree.

Search Within
If you don't have Christmas in your heart,
you won't find it under a tree.

Keeping your mouth shut
prevents a lot of ignorance
from leaking out.

Tight Security
Keeping your mouth shut
prevents a lot of ignorance
from leaking out.

Keeping your mouth shut prevents a lot of
ignorance from leaking out.

Tight Security
Keeping your mouth shut prevents a lot of
ignorance from leaking out.

2

Bible Verses

My help cometh from the LORD, which made heaven and earth (Ps. 121:2).

The Creator's Help
My help cometh from the LORD, which made heaven and earth (Ps. 121:2).

My help cometh from the LORD, which made heaven and earth (Ps. 121:2).

The Creator's Help
My help cometh from the LORD, which made heaven and earth (Ps. 121:2).

And why call ye me, Lord, Lord, and do not the things which I say? (Luke 6:46)

Vain Words
And why call ye me, Lord, Lord, and do not the things which I say? (Luke 6:46)

And why call ye me, Lord, Lord, and do not the things which I say? (Luke 6:46)

Vain Words
And why call ye me, Lord, Lord, and do not the things which I say? (Luke 6:46)

Blessed be the Lord, who daily loadeth us with benefits (Ps. 68:19).

Daily Benefits
Blessed be the Lord, who daily loadeth us with benefits (Ps. 68:19).

Blessed be the Lord, who daily loadeth us with benefits (Ps. 68:19).

Daily Benefits
Blessed be the Lord, who daily loadeth us with benefits (Ps. 68:19).

While we were yet sinners, Christ died for us (Rom. 5:8).

Even in Our Sin
While we were yet sinners, Christ died for us (Rom. 5:8).

While we were yet sinners, Christ died for us (Rom. 5:8).

Even in Our Sin
While we were yet sinners, Christ died for us (Rom. 5:8).

And now abideth faith, hope, charity . . . but the greatest of these is charity (1 Cor. 13:13).

The Greatest
And now abideth faith, hope, charity . . . but the greatest of these is charity (1 Cor. 13:13).

And now abideth faith, hope, charity . . . but the greatest of these is charity (1 Cor. 13:13).

The Greatest
And now abideth faith, hope, charity . . . but the greatest of these is charity (1 Cor. 13:13).

Our soul waiteth for the LORD: he is our help and our shield (Ps. 33:20).

Our Help and Shield
Our soul waiteth for the LORD: he is our help and our shield (Ps. 33:20).

Our soul waiteth for the LORD: he is our help and our shield (Ps. 33:20).

Our Help and Shield
Our soul waiteth for the LORD: he is our help and our shield (Ps. 33:20).

Being justified by faith, we have peace with God through our Lord Jesus Christ (Rom. 5:1).

Peace Through Christ
Being justified by faith, we have peace with God through our Lord Jesus Christ (Rom. 5:1).

Being justified by faith, we have peace with God through our Lord Jesus Christ (Rom. 5:1).

Peace Through Christ
Being justified by faith, we have peace with God through our Lord Jesus Christ (Rom. 5:1).

As far as the east is from the west, so far hath he removed our transgressions from us (Ps. 103:12).

From Sky to Sky
As far as the east is from the west, so far hath he removed our transgressions from us (Ps. 103:12).

As far as the east is from the west, so far hath he removed our transgressions from us (Ps. 103:12).

From Sky to Sky
As far as the east is from the west, so far hath he removed our transgressions from us (Ps. 103:12).

Where the Spirit of the
Lord is, there is liberty
(2 Cor. 3:17).

Lord of Liberty
Where the Spirit of the
Lord is, there is liberty
(2 Cor. 3:17).

Where the Spirit of the Lord is, there is liberty (2 Cor. 3:17).

Lord of Liberty
Where the Spirit of the Lord is, there is liberty (2 Cor. 3:17).

Where two or three are
gathered together in
my name, there am I in
the midst of them
(Matt. 18:20).

In Our Midst
Where two or three are
gathered together in my
name, there am I in the
midst of them (Matt. 18:20).

Where two or three are gathered together in my name,
there am I in the midst of them (Matt. 18:20).

In Our Midst
Where two or three are gathered together in my name,
there am I in the midst of them (Matt. 18:20).

Great is the LORD, and
greatly to be praised
(Ps. 48:1).

Praise Him!
Great is the LORD, and
greatly to be praised
(Ps. 48:1).

Great is the LORD, and greatly to be praised (Ps. 48:1).

Praise Him!
Great is the LORD, and greatly to be praised (Ps. 48:1).

Ye are my friends, if ye do whatsoever I command you (John 15:14).

Friends Indeed
Ye are my friends, if ye do whatsoever I command you (John 15:14).

Ye are my friends, if ye do whatsoever I command you (John 15:14).

Friends Indeed
Ye are my friends, if ye do whatsoever I command you (John 15:14).

For ye are all the children of God by faith in Christ Jesus (Gal. 3:26).

Children by Faith
For ye are all the children of God by faith in Christ Jesus (Gal. 3:26).

For ye are all the children of God by faith in Christ Jesus (Gal. 3:26).

Children by Faith
For ye are all the children of God by faith in Christ Jesus (Gal. 3:26).

O LORD our Lord, how excellent is thy name in all the earth! (Ps. 8:1).

How Excellent!
O LORD our Lord, how excellent is thy name in all the earth! (Ps. 8:1).

O LORD our Lord, how excellent is thy name in all the earth! (Ps. 8:1).

How Excellent!
O LORD our Lord, how excellent is thy name in all the earth! (Ps. 8:1).

For as many as are led
by the Spirit of God,
they are the sons of
God (Rom. 8:14).

Led by His Spirit
For as many as are led
by the Spirit of God,
they are the sons of
God (Rom. 8:14).

For as many as are led by the Spirit of God,
they are the sons of God (Rom. 8:14).

Led by His Spirit
For as many as are led by the Spirit of God,
they are the sons of God (Rom. 8:14).

I press toward the mark
for the prize of the high
calling of God in Christ
Jesus (Phil. 3:14).

Worthy Prize
I press toward the mark
for the prize of the high
calling of God in Christ
Jesus (Phil. 3:14).

I press toward the mark for the prize of the high
calling of God in Christ Jesus (Phil. 3:14).

Worthy Prize
I press toward the mark for the prize of the high
calling of God in Christ Jesus (Phil. 3:14).

The LORD reigneth; let the
earth rejoice (Ps. 97:1).

Rejoice!
The LORD reigneth; let the
earth rejoice (Ps. 97:1).

The LORD reigneth; let the earth rejoice (Ps. 97:1).

Rejoice!
The LORD reigneth; let the earth rejoice (Ps. 97:1).

55

Be not overcome of evil, but overcome evil with good (Rom. 12:21).

Overcome with Good
Be not overcome of evil, but overcome evil with good (Rom. 12:21).

Be not overcome of evil, but overcome evil with good (Rom. 12:21).

Overcome with Good
Be not overcome of evil, but overcome evil with good (Rom. 12:21).

Let the word of Christ dwell in you richly in all wisdom (Col. 3:16).

Christ in Us
Let the word of Christ dwell in you richly in all wisdom (Col. 3:16).

Let the word of Christ dwell in you richly in all wisdom (Col. 3:16).

Christ in Us
Let the word of Christ dwell in you richly in all wisdom (Col. 3:16).

Preserve me, O God: for in thee do I put my trust (Ps. 16:1).

Preservation
Preserve me, O God: for in thee do I put my trust (Ps. 16:1).

Preserve me, O God: for in thee do I put my trust (Ps. 16:1).

Preservation
Preserve me, O God: for in thee do I put my trust (Ps. 16:1).

Bear ye one another's burdens, and so fulfil the law of Christ (Gal. 6:2).

Burden Bearers
Bear ye one another's burdens, and so fulfil the law of Christ (Gal. 6:2).

Bear ye one another's burdens, and so fulfil the law of Christ (Gal. 6:2).

Burden Bearers
Bear ye one another's burdens, and so fulfil the law of Christ (Gal. 6:2).

Ye are the light of the world (Matt. 5:14).

Light in Darkness
Ye are the light of the world (Matt. 5:14).

Ye are the light of the world (Matt. 5:14).

Light in Darkness
Ye are the light of the world (Matt. 5:14).

Serve the LORD with gladness: come before his presence with singing (Ps. 100:2).

Serve with Gladness
Serve the LORD with gladness: come before his presence with singing (Ps. 100:2).

Serve the LORD with gladness: come before his presence with singing (Ps. 100:2).

Serve with Gladness
Serve the LORD with gladness: come before his presence with singing (Ps. 100:2).

Even so faith, if it hath not
works, is dead, being alone
(James 2:17).

Dead Faith
Even so faith, if it hath not
works, is dead, being alone
(James 2:17).

Even so faith, if it hath not works, is
dead, being alone (James 2:17).

Dead Faith
Even so faith, if it hath not works, is
dead, being alone (James 2:17).

In all thy ways acknowledge
him, and he shall direct thy
paths (Prov. 3:6).

Sure Direction
In all thy ways acknowledge
him, and he shall direct thy
paths (Prov. 3:6).

In all thy ways acknowledge him, and he
shall direct thy paths (Prov. 3:6).

Sure Direction
In all thy ways acknowledge him, and he
shall direct thy paths (Prov. 3:6).

Ask, and it shall be given
you; seek, and ye shall find
(Matt. 7:7).

Ask, Seek, Find
Ask, and it shall be given
you; seek, and ye shall find
(Matt. 7:7).

Ask, and it shall be given you; seek,
and ye shall find (Matt. 7:7).

Ask, Seek, Find
Ask, and it shall be given you; seek,
and ye shall find (Matt. 7:7).

The LORD is far from the wicked, but he heareth the prayer of the righteous (Prov. 15:29).

Near Enough to Hear
The LORD is far from the wicked, but he heareth the prayer of the righteous (Prov. 15:29).

The LORD is far from the wicked, but he heareth the prayer of the righteous (Prov. 15:29).

Near Enough to Hear
The LORD is far from the wicked, but he heareth the prayer of the righteous (Prov. 15:29).

Cast thy burden upon the LORD, and he shall sustain thee (Ps. 55:22).

Burden Bearer
Cast thy burden upon the LORD, and he shall sustain thee (Ps. 55:22).

Cast thy burden upon the LORD, and he shall sustain thee (Ps. 55:22).

Burden Bearer
Cast thy burden upon the LORD, and he shall sustain thee (Ps. 55:22).

Grow in grace, and in the knowledge of our Lord and Saviour Jesus Christ (2 Peter 3:18).

Grace and Knowledge
Grow in grace, and in the knowledge of our Lord and Saviour Jesus Christ (2 Peter 3:18).

Grow in grace, and in the knowledge of our Lord and Saviour Jesus Christ (2 Peter 3:18).

Grace and Knowledge
Grow in grace, and in the knowledge of our Lord and Saviour Jesus Christ (2 Peter 3:18).

O give thanks unto the
LORD; for he is good
(Ps. 106:1).

Thanksgiving
O give thanks unto the
LORD; for he is good
(Ps. 106:1).

O give thanks unto the LORD; for he is good (Ps. 106:1).

Thanksgiving
O give thanks unto the LORD; for he is good (Ps. 106:1).

Faith is the substance of
things hoped for, the
evidence of things not seen
(Heb. 11:1).

Faith Defined
Faith is the substance of
things hoped for, the
evidence of things not seen
(Heb. 11:1).

Faith is the substance of things hoped for, the
evidence of things not seen (Heb. 11:1).

Faith Defined
Faith is the substance of things hoped for, the
evidence of things not seen (Heb. 11:1).

The gift of God is eternal
life through Jesus Christ
our Lord (Rom. 6:23).

God's Good Gift
The gift of God is eternal
life through Jesus Christ
our Lord (Rom. 6:23).

The gift of God is eternal life through Jesus
Christ our Lord (Rom. 6:23).

God's Good Gift
The gift of God is eternal life through
Jesus Christ our Lord (Rom. 6:23).

Let thy mercy, O LORD, be upon us, according as we hope in thee (Ps. 33:22).

The Lord's Mercy
Let thy mercy, O LORD, be upon us, according as we hope in thee (Ps. 33:22).

Let thy mercy, O LORD, be upon us, according as we hope in thee (Ps. 33:22).

The Lord's Mercy
Let thy mercy, O LORD, be upon us, according as we hope in thee (Ps. 33:22).

He that believeth on the Son hath everlasting life (John 3:36).

Life Everlasting
He that believeth on the Son hath everlasting life (John 3:36).

He that believeth on the Son hath everlasting life (John 3:36).

Life Everlasting
He that believeth on the Son hath everlasting life (John 3:36).

Thou hast been a shelter for me, and a strong tower from the enemy (Ps. 61:3).

God My Refuge
Thou hast been a shelter for me, and a strong tower from the enemy (Ps. 61:3).

Thou hast been a shelter for me, and a strong tower from the enemy (Ps. 61:3).

God My Refuge
Thou hast been a shelter for me, and a strong tower from the enemy (Ps. 61:3).

I can do all things through Christ which strength-eneth me (Phil. 4:13).

Strength in Christ
I can do all things through Christ which strength-eneth me (Phil. 4:13).

I can do all things through Christ which strengtheneth me (Phil. 4:13).

Strength in Christ
I can do all things through Christ which strengtheneth me (Phil. 4:13).

In all these things we are more than conquerors through him that loved us (Rom. 8:37).

More than Conquerors
In all these things we are more than conquerors through him that loved us (Rom. 8:37).

In all these things we are more than conquerors through him that loved us (Rom. 8:37).

More than Conquerors
In all these things we are more than conquerors through him that loved us (Rom. 8:37).

It is better to trust in the LORD than to put confidence in man (Ps. 118:8).

A Better Trust
It is better to trust in the LORD than to put confidence in man (Ps. 118:8).

It is better to trust in the LORD than to put confidence in man (Ps. 118:8).

A Better Trust
It is better to trust in the LORD than to put confidence in man (Ps. 118:8).

Heaven and earth shall
pass away; but my words
shall not pass away
(Mark 13:31).

Eternal Words
Heaven and earth shal!
pass away; but my words
shall not pass away
(Mark 13:31).

Heaven and earth shall pass away; but my words
shall not pass away (Mark 13:31).

Eternal Words
Heaven and earth shall pass away; but my words
shall not pass away (Mark 13:31).

My soul longeth, yea, even
fainteth, for the courts of the
LORD (Ps. 84:2).

Thirsting for God
My soul longeth, yea, even
fainteth, for the courts of the
LORD (Ps. 84:2).

My soul longeth, yea, even fainteth, for
the courts of the LORD (Ps. 84:2).

Thirsting for God
My soul longeth, yea, even fainteth, for
the courts of the LORD (Ps. 84:2).

Thy word is a lamp unto my
feet, and a light unto my
path (Ps. 119:105).

Guiding Light
Thy word is a lamp unto my
feet, and a light unto my
path (Ps. 119:105).

Thy word is a lamp unto my feet, and a
light unto my path (Ps. 119:105).

Guiding Light
Thy word is a lamp unto my feet, and a
light unto my path (Ps. 119:105).

He leadeth me in the paths
of righteousness for his
name's sake (Ps. 23:3).

True Paths
He leadeth me in the paths
of righteousness for his
name's sake (Ps. 23:3).

He leadeth me in the paths of righteousness
for his name's sake (Ps. 23:3).

True Paths
He leadeth me in the paths of righteousness
for his name's sake (Ps. 23:3).

Thy word have I hid in mine
heart, that I might not sin
against thee (Ps. 119:11).

God's Word
Thy word have I hid in mine
heart, that I might not sin
against thee (Ps. 119:11).

Thy word have I hid in mine heart, that I might
not sin against thee (Ps. 119:11).

God's Word
Thy word have I hid in mine heart, that I might
not sin against thee (Ps. 119:11).

If God be for us, who can
be against us? (Rom. 8:31).

Who, Indeed?
If God be for us, who can
be against us? (Rom. 8:31).

If God be for us, who can be against us? (Rom. 8:31).

Who, Indeed?
If God be for us, who can be against us? (Rom. 8:31).

God is our refuge and strength, a very present help in trouble (Ps. 46:1).

Our Refuge
God is our refuge and strength, a very present help in trouble (Ps. 46:1).

God is our refuge and strength, a very present help in trouble (Ps. 46:1).

Our Refuge
God is our refuge and strength, a very present help in trouble (Ps. 46:1).

The LORD is my light and my salvation; whom shall I fear? (Ps. 27:1).

Prescription for Fear
The LORD is my light and my salvation; whom shall I fear? (Ps. 27:1).

The LORD is my light and my salvation; whom shall I fear? (Ps. 27:1).

Prescription for Fear
The LORD is my light and my salvation; whom shall I fear? (Ps. 27:1).

Finally, my brethren, be strong in the Lord, and in the power of his might (Eph. 6:10).

Strong in the Lord
Finally, my brethren, be strong in the Lord, and in the power of his might (Eph. 6:10).

Finally, my brethren, be strong in the Lord, and in the power of his might (Eph. 6:10).

Strong in the Lord
Finally, my brethren, be strong in the Lord, and in the power of his might (Eph. 6:10).

A soft answer turneth away wrath: but grievous words stir up anger (Prov. 15:1).

Powerful Words
A soft answer turneth away wrath: but grievous words stir up anger (Prov. 15:1).

A soft answer turneth away wrath: but grievous words stir up anger (Prov. 15:1).

Powerful Words
A soft answer turneth away wrath: but grievous words stir up anger (Prov. 15:1).

Let this mind be in you, which was also in Christ Jesus (Phil. 2:5).

Mind of Christ
Let this mind be in you, which was also in Christ Jesus (Phil. 2:5).

Let this mind be in you, which was also in Christ Jesus (Phil. 2:5).

Mind of Christ
Let this mind be in you, which was also in Christ Jesus (Phil. 2:5).

He shall strengthen your heart, all ye that hope in the LORD (Ps. 31:24).

Strength and Hope
He shall strengthen your heart, all ye that hope in the LORD (Ps. 31:24).

He shall strengthen your heart, all ye that hope in the LORD (Ps. 31:24).

Strength and Hope
He shall strengthen your heart, all ye that hope in the LORD (Ps. 31:24).

For God is not the author of confusion, but of peace (1 Cor. 14:33).

Author of Peace
For God is not the author of confusion, but of peace (1 Cor. 14:33).

For God is not the author of confusion, but of peace (1 Cor. 14:33).

Author of Peace
For God is not the author of confusion, but of peace (1 Cor. 14:33).

If we confess our sins, he is faithful and just to forgive us our sins (1 John 1:9).

Results of Confession
If we confess our sins, he is faithful and just to forgive us our sins (1 John 1:9).

If we confess our sins, he is faithful and just to forgive us our sins (1 John 1:9).

Results of Confession
If we confess our sins, he is faithful and just to forgive us our sins (1 John 1:9).

Search me, O God, and know my heart; try me, and know my thoughts (Ps. 139:23).

Heart Searcher
Search me, O God, and know my heart; try me, and know my thoughts (Ps. 139:23).

Search me, O God, and know my heart; try me, and know my thoughts (Ps. 139:23).

Heart Searcher
Search me, O God, and know my heart; try me, and know my thoughts (Ps. 139:23).

79

Blessed are they that mourn: for they shall be comforted (Matt. 5:4).

Blessed Comfort
Blessed are they that mourn: for they shall be comforted (Matt. 5:4).

Blessed are they that mourn: for they shall be comforted (Matt. 5:4).

Blessed Comfort
Blessed are they that mourn: for they shall be comforted (Matt. 5:4).

Where there is no vision, the people perish (Prov. 29:18).

Vision Needed
Where there is no vision, the people perish (Prov. 29:18).

Where there is no vision, the people perish (Prov. 29:18).

Vision Needed
Where there is no vision, the people perish (Prov. 29:18).

So then faith cometh by hearing, and hearing by the word of God (Rom. 10:17).

Faith by Hearing
So then faith cometh by hearing, and hearing by the word of God (Rom. 10:17).

So then faith cometh by hearing, and hearing by the word of God (Rom. 10:17).

Faith by Hearing
So then faith cometh by hearing, and hearing by the word of God (Rom. 10:17).

He healeth the broken in heart, and bindeth up their wounds (Ps. 147:3).

Great Healer
He healeth the broken in heart, and bindeth up their wounds (Ps. 147:3).

He healeth the broken in heart, and bindeth up their wounds (Ps. 147:3).

Great Healer
He healeth the broken in heart, and bindeth up their wounds (Ps. 147:3).

Blessed is he whose transgression is forgiven, whose sin is covered (Ps. 32:1).

Forgiveness
Blessed is he whose transgression is forgiven, whose sin is covered (Ps. 32:1).

Blessed is he whose transgression is forgiven, whose sin is covered (Ps. 32:1).

Forgiveness
Blessed is he whose transgression is forgiven, whose sin is covered (Ps. 32:1).

The Lord knoweth how to deliver the godly out of temptations (2 Peter 2:9).

Deliverance
The Lord knoweth how to deliver the godly out of temptations (2 Peter 2:9).

The Lord knoweth how to deliver the godly out of temptations (2 Peter 2:9).

Deliverance
The Lord knoweth how to deliver the godly out of temptations (2 Peter 2:9).

They that wait upon the LORD shall renew their strength (Isa. 40:31).

True Renewal
They that wait upon the LORD shall renew their strength (Isa. 40:31).

They that wait upon the LORD shall renew their strength (Isa. 40:31).

True Renewal
They that wait upon the LORD shall renew their strength (Isa. 40:31).

Jesus Christ the same yesterday, and to day, and for ever (Heb. 13:8).

The Unchanging
Jesus Christ the same yesterday, and to day, and for ever (Heb. 13:8).

Jesus Christ the same yesterday, and to day, and for ever (Heb. 13:8).

The Unchanging
Jesus Christ the same yesterday, and to day, and for ever (Heb. 13:8).

The LORD is my shepherd; I shall not want (Ps. 23:1).

Our Shepherd
The LORD is my shepherd; I shall not want (Ps. 23:1).

The LORD is my shepherd; I shall not want (Ps. 23:1).

Our Shepherd
The LORD is my shepherd; I shall not want (Ps. 23:1).

85

Trust in the LORD . . . and lean not unto thine own understanding (Prov. 3:5).

Well-Placed Trust
Trust in the LORD . . . and lean not unto thine own understanding (Prov. 3:5).

Trust in the LORD . . . and lean not unto thine own understanding (Prov. 3:5).

Well-Placed Trust
Trust in the LORD . . . and lean not unto thine own understanding (Prov. 3:5).

I am with you alway, even unto the end of the world (Matt. 28:20).

Promised Presence
I am with you alway, even unto the end of the world (Matt. 28:20).

I am with you alway, even unto the end of the world (Matt. 28:20).

Promised Presence
I am with you alway, even unto the end of the world (Matt. 28:20).

Children, obey your parents in the Lord: for this is right (Eph. 6:1).

The Right Thing
Children, obey your parents in the Lord: for this is right (Eph. 6:1).

Children, obey your parents in the Lord: for this is right (Eph. 6:1).

The Right Thing
Children, obey your parents in the Lord: for this is right (Eph. 6:1).

A good name is better
than precious ointment
(Eccles. 7:1).

Good Reputation
A good name is better
than precious ointment
(Eccles. 7:1).

A good name is better than precious ointment (Eccles. 7:1).

Good Reputation
A good name is better than precious ointment (Eccles. 7:1).

O LORD, thou hast
searched me, and
known me (Ps. 139:1).

Searched and Known
O LORD, thou hast
searched me, and
known me (Ps. 139:1).

O LORD, thou hast searched me, and known me (Ps. 139:1).

Searched and Known
O LORD, thou hast searched me, and known me (Ps. 139:1).

Go ye into all the world, and
preach the gospel to every
creature (Mark 16:15).

All the World
Go ye into all the world, and
preach the gospel to every
creature (Mark 16:15).

Go ye into all the world, and preach the gospel
to every creature (Mark 16:15).

All the World
Go ye into all the world, and preach the gospel
to every creature (Mark 16:15).

3

Interesting Bible Facts

The Book of Joshua describes the conquest of Canaan by the Hebrew people.

Canaan's Conquest
The Book of Joshua describes the conquest of Canaan by the Hebrew people.

The Book of Joshua describes the conquest of Canaan by the Hebrew people.

Canaan's Conquest
The Book of Joshua describes the conquest of Canaan by the Hebrew people.

The New Testament contains more than 30 different quotations from the Book of Deuteronomy.

Deuteronomy Quotations
The New Testament contains more than 30 different quotations from the Book of Deuteronomy.

The New Testament contains more than 30 different quotations from the Book of Deuteronomy.

Deuteronomy Quotations
The New Testament contains more than 30 different quotations from the Book of Deuteronomy.

The King James, or Authorized, Version of the Bible was first published in 1611.

Birth of the KJV
The King James, or Authorized, Version of the Bible was first published in 1611.

The King James, or Authorized, Version of the Bible was first published in 1611.

Birth of the KJV
The King James, or Authorized, Version of the Bible was first published in 1611.

The persons in the Old Testament known as patriarchs are Abraham, Isaac, Jacob, and Joseph.

Four Patriarchs
The persons in the Old Testament known as patriarchs are Abraham, Isaac, Jacob, and Joseph.

The persons in the Old Testament known as patriarchs are Abraham, Isaac, Jacob, and Joseph.

Four Patriarchs
The persons in the Old Testament known as patriarchs are Abraham, Isaac, Jacob, and Joseph.

The Book of Numbers describes the "numbering," or census of the Hebrews in the wilderness.

Wilderness Census
The Book of Numbers describes the "numbering," or census of the Hebrews in the wilderness.

The Book of Numbers describes the "numbering," or census of the Hebrews in the wilderness.

Wilderness Census
The Book of Numbers describes the "numbering," or census of the Hebrews in the wilderness.

The tabernacle was a tent which served as a worship place for the Hebrews in the wilderness.

Tabernacle Worship
The tabernacle was a tent which served as a worship place for the Hebrews in the wilderness.

The tabernacle was a tent which served as a worship place for the Hebrews in the wilderness.

Tabernacle Worship
The tabernacle was a tent which served as a worship place for the Hebrews in the wilderness.

The first of the Ten Commandments is, "Thou shalt have no other gods before me."

First Commandment
The first of the Ten Commandments is, "Thou shalt have no other gods before me."

The first of the Ten Commandments is, "Thou shalt have no other gods before me."

First Commandment
The first of the Ten Commandments is, "Thou shalt have no other gods before me."

As the "book of beginnings" in the Bible, Genesis answers such questions as how the world began.

Book of Beginnings
As the "book of beginnings" in the Bible, Genesis answers such questions as how the world began.

As the "book of beginnings" in the Bible, Genesis answers such questions as how the world began.

Book of Beginnings
As the "book of beginnings" in the Bible, Genesis answers such questions as how the world began.

The New Testament
contains 27 separate books.

27 Books
The New Testament
contains 27 separate books.

The New Testament contains 27 separate books.

27 Books
The New Testament contains 27 separate books.

The Old Testament contains 39 separate books.

39 Books
The Old Testament contains 39 separate books.

The Old Testament contains 39 separate books.

39 Books
The Old Testament contains 39 separate books.

Many early biblical manuscripts were written on papyrus, a form of paper made from a reed-like plant.

Ancient Paper
Many early biblical manuscripts were written on papyrus, a form of paper made from a reed-like plant.

Many early biblical manuscripts were written on papyrus, a form of paper made from a reed-like plant.

Ancient Paper
Many early biblical manuscripts were written on papyrus, a form of paper made from a reed-like plant.

The translation of the Old Testament into Greek during the third century B.C. was known as the Septuagint.

Greek Translation
The translation of the Old Testament into Greek during the third century B.C. was known as the Septuagint.

The translation of the Old Testament into Greek during the third century B.C. was known as the Septuagint.

Greek Translation
The translation of the Old Testament into Greek during the third century B.C. was known as the Septuagint.

The Dead Sea Scrolls included a copy of the Book of Isaiah from the second century A.D.

Isaiah Scroll
The Dead Sea Scrolls included a copy of the Book of Isaiah from the second century A.D.

The Dead Sea Scrolls included a copy of the Book of Isaiah from the second century A.D.

Isaiah Scroll
The Dead Sea Scrolls included a copy of the Book of Isaiah from the second century A.D.

All the books of the New Testament were written originally in the Greek language.

Written in Greek
All the books of the New Testament were written originally in the Greek language.

All the books of the New Testament were written originally in the Greek language.

Written in Greek
All the books of the New Testament were written originally in the Greek language.

The books of the Old Testament were written originally in either Hebrew or Aramaic.

Hebrew and Aramaic
The books of the Old Testament were written originally in either Hebrew or Aramaic.

The books of the Old Testament were written originally in either Hebrew or Aramaic.

Hebrew and Aramaic
The books of the Old Testament were written originally in either Hebrew or Aramaic.

David was succeeded by his son Solomon as king of Judah.

David and Solomon
David was succeeded by his son Solomon as king of Judah.

David was succeeded by his son Solomon as king of Judah.

David and Solomon
David was succeeded by his son Solomon as king of Judah.

Nehemiah led the Hebrew people to rebuild the walls of Jerusalem after their years as captives in Babylon.

Nehemiah's Wall
Nehemiah led the Hebrew people to rebuild the walls of Jerusalem after their years as captives in Babylon.

Nehemiah led the Hebrew people to rebuild the walls of Jerusalem after their years as captives in Babylon.

Nehemiah's Wall
Nehemiah led the Hebrew people to rebuild the walls of Jerusalem after their years as captives in Babylon.

The Book of Job deals with the question, Why do innocent people suffer?

Eternal Question
The Book of Job deals with the question, Why do innocent people suffer?

The Book of Job deals with the question, Why do innocent people suffer?

Eternal Question
The Book of Job deals with the question, Why do innocent people suffer?

The Book of Psalms is the longest book in the Bible, containing 150 individual psalms.

Longest Book
The Book of Psalms is the longest book in the Bible, containing 150 individual psalms.

The Book of Psalms is the longest book in the Bible, containing 150 individual psalms.

Longest Book
The Book of Psalms is the longest book in the Bible, containing 150 individual psalms.

The psalms were written by many different people across a period of about 500 years.

Many Writers
The psalms were written by many different people across a period of about 500 years.

The psalms were written by many different people across a period of about 500 years.

Many Writers
The psalms were written by many different people across a period of about 500 years.

The 23rd Psalm is known as "the shepherd psalm" because it portrays God as a guiding shepherd.

Shepherd Psalm
The 23rd Psalm is known as "the shepherd psalm" because it portrays God as a guiding shepherd.

The 23rd Psalm is known as "the shepherd psalm" because it portrays God as a guiding shepherd.

Shepherd Psalm
The 23rd Psalm is known as "the shepherd psalm" because it portrays God as a guiding shepherd.

The theme of the Book of Proverbs is godly wisdom.

Godly Wisdom
The theme of the Book of Proverbs is godly wisdom.

The theme of the Book of Proverbs is godly wisdom.

Godly Wisdom
The theme of the Book of Proverbs is godly wisdom.

The Old Testament books classified as wisdom literature are Job, Proverbs, and Ecclesiastes.

Wisdom Books
The Old Testament books classified as wisdom literature are Job, Proverbs, and Ecclesiastes.

The Old Testament books classified as wisdom literature are Job, Proverbs, and Ecclesiastes.

Wisdom Books
The Old Testament books classified as wisdom literature are Job, Proverbs, and Ecclesiastes.

The central personality
in the Book of 2 Samuel
is King David.

David In Samuel
The central personality
in the Book of 2 Samuel
is King David.

The central personality in the Book of 2 Samuel is King David.

David In Samuel
The central personality in the Book of 2 Samuel is King David.

The shortest book in the
Old Testament is Obadiah,
containing only 21 verses.

A 21-Verse Book
The shortest book in the
Old Testament is Obadiah,
containing only 21 verses.

The shortest book in the Old Testament is
Obadiah, containing only 21 verses.

A 21-Verse Book
The shortest book in the Old Testament is
Obadiah, containing only 21 verses.

Jeremiah is called the
"weeping prophet" because
of his sorrow over the sins
of his people.

The "Weeping Prophet"
Jeremiah is called the
"weeping prophet" because
of his sorrow over the sins
of his people.

Jeremiah is called the "weeping prophet" because
of his sorrow over the sins of his people.

The "Weeping Prophet"
Jeremiah is called the "weeping prophet" because
of his sorrow over the sins of his people.

The Book of Lamentations expresses despair over the destruction of Jerusalem by an invading army.

Despair in the City
The Book of Lamentations expresses despair over the destruction of Jerusalem by an invading army.

The Book of Lamentations expresses despair over the destruction of Jerusalem by an invading army.

Despair in the City
The Book of Lamentations expresses despair over the destruction of Jerusalem by an invading army.

The earthly ministry of Jesus lasted about three years.

3-Year Ministry
The earthly ministry of Jesus lasted about three years.

The earthly ministry of Jesus lasted about three years.

3-Year Ministry
The earthly ministry of Jesus lasted about three years.

On his third missionary journey, the apostle Paul spent nearly three years in the city of Ephesus.

Paul in Ephesus
On his third missionary journey, the apostle Paul spent nearly three years in the city of Ephesus.

On his third missionary journey, the apostle Paul spent nearly three years in the city of Ephesus.

Paul in Ephesus
On his third missionary journey, the apostle Paul spent nearly three years in the city of Ephesus.

The first temple in
Jerusalem was built during
the reign of Solomon,
about 950 B.C.

First Temple
The first temple in
Jerusalem was built during
the reign of Solomon,
about 950 B.C.

The first temple in Jerusalem was built during
the reign of Solomon, about 950 B.C.

First Temple
The first temple in Jerusalem was built during
the reign of Solomon, about 950 B.C.

Mark, the first gospel to be
written, portrays Jesus as a
person of action and power.

Gospel of Action
Mark, the first gospel to be
written, portrays Jesus as a
person of action and power.

Mark, the first gospel to be written, portrays
Jesus as a person of action and power.

Gospel of Action
Mark, the first gospel to be written, portrays
Jesus as a person of action and power.

After his conversion to
Christianity, Saul's name
was changed to Paul.

From Saul to Paul
After his conversion to
Christianity, Saul's name
was changed to Paul.

After his conversion to Christianity, Saul's
name was changed to Paul.

From Saul to Paul
After his conversion to Christianity, Saul's
name was changed to Paul.

The four Old Testament books known as the major prophets are Isaiah, Jeremiah, Ezekiel, and Daniel.

Major Prophets
The four Old Testament books known as the major prophets are Isaiah, Jeremiah, Ezekiel, and Daniel.

The four Old Testament books known as the major prophets are Isaiah, Jeremiah, Ezekiel, and Daniel.

Major Prophets
The four Old Testament books known as the major prophets are Isaiah, Jeremiah, Ezekiel, and Daniel.

John is called "the gospel of belief" since "to believe" appears about 100 times in this book.

Book of Belief
John is called "the gospel of belief" since "to believe" appears about 100 times in this book.

John is called "the gospel of belief" since "to believe" appears about 100 times in this book.

Book of Belief
John is called "the gospel of belief" since "to believe" appears about 100 times in this book.

Acts describes the rapid spread of Christianity throughout the world during the first century A.D.

Christianity's Spread
Acts describes the rapid spread of Christianity throughout the world during the first century A.D.

Acts describes the rapid spread of Christianity throughout the world during the first century A.D.

Christianity's Spread
Acts describes the rapid spread of Christianity throughout the world during the first century A.D.

The Gospel of Matthew focuses on Jesus as the fulfillment of Old Testament prophecy.

Matthew's Focus
The Gospel of Matthew focuses on Jesus as the fulfillment of Old Testament prophecy.

The Gospel of Matthew focuses on Jesus as the fulfillment of Old Testament prophecy.

Matthew's Focus
The Gospel of Matthew focuses on Jesus as the fulfillment of Old Testament prophecy.

The word "Bible" comes from the Greek word *biblos,* which means "book."

***Biblos* = Book**
The word "Bible" comes from the Greek word *biblos,* which means "book."

The word "Bible" comes from the Greek word *biblos,* which means "book."

***Biblos* = Book**
The word "Bible" comes from the Greek word *biblos,* which means "book."

The first book printed by movable type was the Gutenberg Bible, printed in Germany in 1456.

Gutenberg Bible
The first book printed by movable type was the Gutenberg Bible, printed in Germany in 1456.

The first book printed by movable type was the Gutenberg Bible, printed in Germany in 1456.

Gutenberg Bible
The first book printed by movable type was the Gutenberg Bible, printed in Germany in 1456.

The New Testament contains about 180 direct quotations from the Old Testament.

Bible Quotations
The New Testament contains about 180 direct quotations from the Old Testament.

The New Testament contains about 180 direct quotations from the Old Testament.

Bible Quotations
The New Testament contains about 180 direct quotations from the Old Testament.

About one-third of the Old Testament is written in poetry.

Old Testament Poetry
About one-third of the Old Testament is written in poetry.

About one-third of the Old Testament is written in poetry.

Old Testament Poetry
About one-third of the Old Testament is written in poetry.

David is listed as author of 73 of the 150 psalms in the Book of Psalms.

David in the Psalms
David is listed as author of 73 of the 150 psalms in the Book of Psalms.

David is listed as author of 73 of the 150 psalms in the Book of Psalms.

David in the Psalms
David is listed as author of 73 of the 150 psalms in the Book of Psalms.

The Book of Isaiah is often called the "fifth gospel" because it describes God's purpose of salvation.

Gospel in Isaiah
The Book of Isaiah is often called the "fifth gospel" because it describes God's purpose of salvation.

The Book of Isaiah is often called the "fifth gospel" because it describes God's purpose of salvation.

Gospel in Isaiah
The Book of Isaiah is often called the "fifth gospel" because it describes God's purpose of salvation.

The prophet Micah predicted Jesus would be born in Bethlehem (see Micah 5:2).

Micah's Prediction
The prophet Micah predicted Jesus would be born in Bethlehem (see Micah 5:2).

The prophet Micah predicted Jesus would be born in Bethlehem (see Micah 5:2).

Micah's Prediction
The prophet Micah predicted Jesus would be born in Bethlehem (see Micah 5:2).

Paul's declaration "The just shall live by faith" is a direct quotation from Habakkuk 2:4.

Habakkuk Quotation
Paul's declaration "The just shall live by faith" is a direct quotation from Habakkuk 2:4.

Paul's declaration "The just shall live by faith" is a direct quotation from Habakkuk 2:4.

Habakkuk Quotation
Paul's declaration "The just shall live by faith" is a direct quotation from Habakkuk 2:4.

The four Gospels—Matthew, Mark, Luke, and John—make up almost one-half of the New Testament.

The Important Gospels
The four Gospels—Matthew, Mark, Luke, and John—make up almost one-half of the New Testament.

The four Gospels—Matthew, Mark, Luke, and John—make up almost one-half of the New Testament.

The Important Gospels
The four Gospels—Matthew, Mark, Luke, and John—make up almost one-half of the New Testament.

Jesus' Sermon on the Mount is found in the Gospel of Matthew (chaps. 5–7).

Sermon in Matthew
Jesus' Sermon on the Mount is found in the Gospel of Matthew (chaps. 5–7).

Jesus' Sermon on the Mount is found in the Gospel of Matthew (chaps. 5–7).

Sermon in Matthew
Jesus' Sermon on the Mount is found in the Gospel of Matthew (chaps. 5–7).

The Gospel of Matthew quotes more from the Old Testament than any of the other Gospels.

Quotations in Matthew
The Gospel of Matthew quotes more from the Old Testament than any of the other Gospels.

The Gospel of Matthew quotes more from the Old Testament than any of the other Gospels.

Quotations in Matthew
The Gospel of Matthew quotes more from the Old Testament than any of the other Gospels.

Mark is the shortest of the four Gospels, containing only 16 chapters.

Shortest Gospel
Mark is the shortest of the four Gospels, containing only 16 chapters.

Mark is the shortest of the four Gospels, containing only 16 chapters.

Shortest Gospel
Mark is the shortest of the four Gospels, containing only 16 chapters.

The Holy Spirit is mentioned almost 60 times in the Book of Acts.

Holy Spirit in Acts
The Holy Spirit is mentioned almost 60 times in the Book of Acts.

The Holy Spirit is mentioned almost 60 times in the Book of Acts.

Holy Spirit in Acts
The Holy Spirit is mentioned almost 60 times in the Book of Acts.

Nine letters of Paul in the New Testament were addressed to churches and four to individuals.

Paul's Letters
Nine letters of Paul in the New Testament were addressed to churches and four to individuals.

Nine letters of Paul in the New Testament were addressed to churches and four to individuals.

Paul's Letters
Nine letters of Paul in the New Testament were addressed to churches and four to individuals.

The Bible is God's guide
for the Christian life.
Read it regularly.

Christian Guide
The Bible is God's
guide for the Christian
life. Read it regularly.

The Bible is God's guide for the Christian life. Read it regularly.

Christian Guide
The Bible is God's guide for the Christian life. Read it regularly.

The Book of Psalms is
one of the most widely
read and universally used
books in the Bible.

Popular Book
The Book of Psalms is
one of the most widely
read and universally
used books in the Bible.

The Book of Psalms is one of the most widely read and
universally used books in the Bible.

Popular Book
The Book of Psalms is one of the most widely read and
universally used books in the Bible.

Before the invention of
printing all copies of the
Bible were produced
laboriously by hand.

Handmade
Before the invention of
printing all copies of the
Bible were produced
laboriously by hand.

Before the invention of printing all copies of the
Bible were produced laboriously by hand.

Handmade
Before the invention of printing all copies of the
Bible were produced laboriously by hand.

125

The three best-known judges in the Book of Judges are Deborah, Gideon, and Samson.

Famous Judges
The three best-known judges in the Book of Judges are Deborah, Gideon, and Samson.

The three best-known judges in the Book of Judges are Deborah, Gideon, and Samson.

Famous Judges
The three best-known judges in the Book of Judges are Deborah, Gideon, and Samson.

Abraham, because of his obedience and faithfulness, was called "the Friend of God" (James 2:23).

God's Friend
Abraham, because of his obedience and faithfulness, was called "the Friend of God" (James 2:23).

Abraham, because of his obedience and faithfulness, was called "the Friend of God" (James 2:23).

God's Friend
Abraham, because of his obedience and faithfulness, was called "the Friend of God" (James 2:23).

A major emphasis of the Book of Leviticus is holiness: "ye shall be holy; for I am holy" (Lev. 11:44).

Holiness in Leviticus
A major emphasis of the Book of Leviticus is holiness: "ye shall be holy; for I am holy" (Lev. 11:44).

A major emphasis of the Book of Leviticus is holiness: "ye shall be holy; for I am holy" (Lev. 11:44).

Holiness in Leviticus
A major emphasis of the Book of Leviticus is holiness: "ye shall be holy; for I am holy" (Lev. 11:44).